Story B▮▮▮▮ ▮▮▮▮▮▮

and The Haunted Studio

By **Yolanda King**
Pictures By **Pia Reyes**

Story Bird Dance

and The Haunted Studio

Summary: Something's going on in this house... Sky, Jada and Nia love their dance studio and their instructor, Ms. Kenya. But when they learn that their studio is being moved to an empty old house, their excitement turns to dread. While exploring the house's second floor, they encounter a ghost! They have to get rid of the ghost before the other students find out it exist.

ISBN 978-0-9910272-6-2

TANGLED
PRESS

www.TangledPress.com

Don't miss the second Story Bird Dance book

Story Bird Dance
and the Snowbird Ballet

Table of Contents

Chapter One
Legacy

"Come on, Jada!" Sky ran down the sidewalk, her blue backpack banging against her back.

Jada trailed behind doing a slow *pirouette*. "It's not like Ms. Kenya is going to start without us," she said, chewing absently on one of her French braids.

Sky glared at her. "She said she had news for us! Hurry!"

Jada sighed and sped up.

It was the beginning of the new dance season, and they were both excited about being able to dance again. A new season meant shiny wooden floors, sparkling mirrors and hard work. The last season ended with the most exciting recital. The dances and *backdrops* represented Earth, Wind, Fire and Water. The costumes, colors, and dances matched the Elements theme. What other announcement could Ms. Kenya have for them? The recital theme was a big deal.

Nia was waiting for them at the front doors of their dance studio, taking out her sparkling purple earrings. Her matching skateboard leaned against the wall next to her.

"What's the hurry? The yoga class hasn't even ended yet," Nia said, regarding her friends with a smirk.

Sky planted her hands on her hips, her wild cocoa curls making her look like a lion. "Ms. Kenya emailed my

mom saying she had big news for us," Sky said.

Nia shrugged, her cat-style glasses slipping down her nose. "Maybe she's picked out this year's theme already," Nia said.

Jada clapped her hands. "I wonder what it's gonna be! Last year was SO awesome!" Jada said.

"The Elements was an EPIC theme, and I looked great in fire red, and the babies looked so cute in sea green blue," said Nia.

The girls walked into the cool foyer of the studio, placed their shoes on the shelves, and went to change into their leotards and tights. Once the entire class was assembled in the airy, mirror-lined room, their teacher, Ms. Kenya, stood in front of them. Her usually smiling face looked worried.

"Lovelies, I have some... news...," she ran a hand through the end of her coily black ponytail.

Sky stood tall in *first position*, her eyebrows crinkling with concern. "What is it, Ms. Kenya? Is there something wrong?" she asked.

Ms. Kenya leaned back against the mirrors. "Everyone... we're moving the studio." A collective gasp rose up from the young dancers.

"To where?" Jada asked.

"Why?" Nia added. Ms. Kenya raised her hands, which usually would have silenced her pupils, but the news had struck them and created complete disorder. She waited until the shrieks died down enough for her to speak.

"Our lease on this building is up, and we have to move. But don't worry, little ones. There's a place for us." The class began to chatter again.

"Where are we moving? Is it far away? Is it a nice place? Are there mirrors?" The questions swirled like thunderclouds from the students' mouths.

"We're *fortunate.* You all remember my old instructor, Mrs. Allen?" Ms. Kenya said. The girls nodded; Mrs. Allen had run the studio before Ms. Kenya.

"Well, she's retired to another state. Her house has been sitting empty for some time now and she generously gave it to us. Mrs. Allen's house will be the new home for Story Bird Dance Academy. She believes you are her *legacy.* I've already spoken with all the parents from each class. It's a big house, and we think it will be perfect for a dance academy," Ms. Kenya said. The girls began to whisper to each other. Now Ms. Kenya was smiling.

"Do you want to see it, girls?" she asked. Ten pairs of beautiful young eyes looked up towards her.

"Yes! Let's go!" they squealed. Ms. Kenya ushered her dancers out to the blue school bus they usually used to get to recitals and competitions. The group settled into their usual seats and pressed their faces eagerly to the windows, watching as the bus took them to the new studio. The bus started slowing down as they passed a small park, library, ice-cream shop, beauty salon and veterinary clinic. They pulled to a stop in front of a towering house in the quiet neighborhood. Everyone stared up at it, and they all started to whisper. The still house had a deep, wide front porch and tall trees in need of pruning. Ms. Kenya stood up at the front of the bus.

"Come on. Let's go check it out!" She followed the stampede of leotards out the bus door and into the house.

A layer of dust covered every surface. "It smells in here," Nia said, wrinkling her nose.

"The wallpaper is ugly," Jada said, touching one of the peeling walls and cringing.

"I think this floor is gonna cave-in if we dance on it," Sky said, tiptoeing along the battered wooden floors. Ms. Kenya knelt in the middle of the students.

"Come on, guys. It'll be nice once we fix it up. Sure, maybe it's been empty for a little bit too long, but once we get some warm bodies in here, some paint, *barres*, floors and mirrors, it'll be perfect." She put her arms around the kids. "This huge gift from Mrs. Allen is a new beginning."

"Yeah, I guess," Jada said.

Nia tugged gently on one of Jada's braids. "It'll be ok, Jada. We'll all help, right guys?" she said. The girls all nodded, and crowded around their dance instructor. Ms. Kenya found a few heads and gently patted and pulled a few curls and braids.

"That's the spirit, my little love-lies. It'll all be all right, you'll see." She stood up. "Do you all want to explore a little bit before we go back to the old studio?" she asked. The girls jumped up and began running from room to room. "Walking feet please," called Ms. Kenya. Sky grabbed Nia and Jada by their hands.

"Come on! Let's check out upstairs." They ran up the narrow staircase and into the gloomy upper floor.

"There are probably dead bugs and stuff up here," Jada said, wrapping her arms around herself.

"Don't be a baby, Jada. Dead bugs can't do anything to us," Nia said.

Jada shrugged. "Doesn't mean they're not gross," she said.

"Jada, really. Check out this room.

It's huge. I could do one hundred *grand jetes* across this floor," said Nia.

Sky shushed them. "Do you guys hear that?"

The girls fell silent so they could listen. At first there was nothing, and then it started—a soft scratching noise coming from somewhere in the walls.

"What's that?" Nia whispered.

"How should I know?" Jada whispered back.

Sky walked close to the wall, placing her ear against the peeling wallpaper and crumbling plaster. "I think it's coming from over here," she said, beckoning her friends to follow her.

As they crept along the hallway, they heard something rustling, and then a sudden whoosh overhead and around them. Jada screamed, and the girls ran back down the stairs, running right into Ms. Kenya.

"Girls, what is it?" she asked. It took them a moment to catch their breath.

"We heard noises. We weren't sure where they were coming from," panted Nia.

"Then something whooshed past

us!" Jada added.

Sky looked up at her dance instructor, brown eyes wide. "This house is haunted!"

Chapter Two

Haunted

"The house is not haunted," Zane said, peeling the crust off of his sandwich. Sky hit his shoulder.

"You weren't there! You didn't

hear the noises," she said. Zane took a long drink from his water bottle and regarded her with a skeptical expression.

"You guys are old enough to know that ghosts don't exist." He turned to Jada and Nia, sitting above them on the bleachers so they could watch the soccer practice. "It's ridiculous."

Nia planted her hands on her hips. "Well, SOMETHING happened up there," she said. Jada nodded in agreement, her mouth full of almond butter.

Zane rolled his honey brown eyes. "So go back and check it out! Ghosts are not real. And if you keep on scaring the other girls, they won't want to move and Ms. Kenya might have to close down the dance studio."

Sky clapped a hand over her mouth. "Ms. Kenya would never close the studio! She can't!" she cried.

Zane shrugged, crumbling his crust and throwing the pieces to a watchful pigeon. "That's what I heard mom saying last night. Buildings are expensive. I don't think Ms. Kenya can afford to move the studio anywhere else."

Jada finally finished chewing. "So,

we're all going to have to stop dancing with Ms. Kenya?" she asked.

Sky shook her head fiercely. "No. We can't let a haunted house close the studio. Ms. Kenya has worked so hard," she said.

Lola jogged up to them, her soccer bag over her shoulder. "What's this about a haunted house?" she asked, twirling a few braids around her finger.

"We think that the house that Ms. Kenya wants to move the studio to is haunted," Nia explained.

Lola sat down beside Sky, pulling

a bag of carrots out of her backpack. "Is that what you guys were doing upstairs?" she asked. "Bummer. That old house has so much space. Ms. Kenya could have lots of classes at one time. And the backyard is perfect for tag or hide and go seek. What are you going to do?"

Sky exchanged a look with her friends. "We have to get rid of the ghost or no one will want to dance at Story Bird."

Chapter Three

Upstairs

"I can't believe I let you talk me into this," Jada said as they stood on the front porch of the house.

"I can't believe my mom even let me do this," Nia added, clutching her skateboard to her chest like a teddy bear.

"Come on. Do you want to save the studio or not?" Sky asked. She reached out and pushed the door open, revealing the mostly dark foyer. The girls all peered into the gloom, and then looked at each other.

Nia gestured at Sky. "This was your idea. You go first," she said.

Sky swallowed, and then tiptoed into the house. They crept around the foyer, Jada shining light into the corners with a flashlight she had borrowed from her dad.

"I think we should go back up-stairs," Nia whispered.

"To hang out with the dead bugs and the ghost? No way!" Jada said, chomping furiously on her braid like she always did when she was nervous.

"Well, we're not finding anything down here. Remember Ms. Kenya and the other girls stayed downstairs for the tour and they didn't find anything scarier than a dust bunny," Sky hissed. They all looked up the stairs at the dark entrance to the second floor.

Jada took a big step back. "Maybe

we should just tell our parents and let them investigate," she said.

Nia waved her hand in front of Jada's face. "Hello? Wake up, Jada! You know that grown-ups believe in ghosts even less than kids do! They'd never believe us!" she said.

Jada shoved her hands into the pockets of her sweater. "You're right. But if we get vanished by an angry ghost, I'm going to blame you two," she said.

As they began to creep up the stairs, they heard the front door bang open. They all screamed. Jada threw her arms around Sky for protection.

"Hey guys, am I too late for the ghost hunt?" Zane appeared at the bottom of the stairs. He studied them with his head cocked. "What's up with you? You all look like you've seen a ghost."

Nia shook her head indignantly, her fear melting away. "You scared us, you sneak! What are you even doing here, anyway?" she asked.

Zane shrugged. "I like Ms. Kenya as much as you do. Coach says her dance classes are helping with my soccer skills. I thought I could help," he said.

The girls looked at each other, considering his proposal. They pressed against the walls of the stairway to let their friend get through.

"Well, in that case, you can go up first," Nia said.

Chapter Four

Investigate

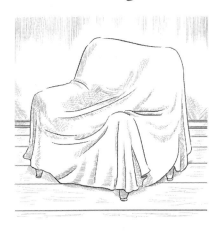

"This place really is a dump," Zane said as he stood in the middle of the first empty room.

The girls stood in the doorway, each secretly keeping an eye on the hallway as well as the room.

"Yeah, we know. Ms. Kenya says

she'll have to fix it up," Jada said.

Nia pushed her glasses up her nose. "Where do you think we'd find the ghost?" she asked. Jada wanted to be anywhere but here. "Let's try looking in the front yard. If I were a ghost, I'd want to be in a wide open space not some scary old house," she offered.

Zane scratched his head. "I started watching a bunch of ghost catcher movies. I don't think they really hide. I think they just disappear and reappear where they want," he said.

"Great. Hide and seek with something that can disappear," Jada said bitterly.

Sky poked her in the side. "Don't be grumpy. It's gotta be here somewhere," she said.

"How do we know it's just one ghost?" asked Jada.

"That's an even bigger problem," sighed Sky. They all looked around the room and peered into the hallway.

"Should we check the other rooms?" Zane said.

"Probably. If I had to stay in this house, I wouldn't just haunt one room," Jada said. They went and checked the other rooms. Most of them were empty; one or two of them had a couple of pieces of furniture covered in sheets. Mostly, the top floor was filled with dust.

Zane peeked underneath a sheet and wrinkled his nose. "All of this stuff smells like mothballs," he said.

Nia pinched her nose. "This is all so gross. Why did we come here again?" she asked.

Sky shot her a glare. "Stick to the plan, Nia. We need to help Ms. Kenya," she said.

Nia glared back, but didn't say

anything.

They entered the room at the end of the hall. This room had much more furniture in it than the rest, and all of it was draped in off-white sheets, giving the place an eerie feel.

Jada tugged on the strap of Sky's backpack. "Let's go, guys. It's creepy in here."

Sky swallowed the lump in her throat. "Let's just check this room out. Then we can go home, alright?" she said. The others nodded.

Zane climbed through the tangle of sheets and furniture and checked

underneath table legs and inside closets.

"I don't see anything, guys," he said as he came back to the doorway. As they turned to leave, they heard that same scratching noise that they had heard the first time.

"There it is! The ghost!" Jada whispered, grabbing Nia's arm. The kids froze, listening as the scratching moved around the room.

"You guys weren't kidding. This is really scary stuff," Zane whispered.

As they stared into the room, one of the sheets began to wiggle and move on the chair that it draped.

"THE GHOST!" Nia screamed.

The kids ran for the stairs, tripping and falling over each other. Just as Nia was reaching the bottom of the stairs, she tripped and scraped her knee.

"Nia?! Are you ok?" Sky's breathless voice called up for her.

"Yeah, it hurts a little" she said. She put her arms around Sky and Jada. Her friends helped her limp out of the house and sat down on the edge of the sidewalk. Jada inspected Nia's knee, which was coated with blood and dust from the floor of the house.

"We should go home and get your mom to clean this up," said Jada. The kids nodded.

Zane hugged himself, even though the day was warm. "And then we should talk about what we're going to do about the ghost."

Chapter Five

Surprise

The next day, the kids went to the studio for some of their last classes before the move. None of them felt very good about it. After all, they were sure that there was a ghost in that house. Everyone headed to the barre as the music began.

"All right loves. Let's begin," said Ms. Kenya. "Five, six, seven, eight and *plié* two, three, four. Up five, six, seven, eight... again, pull up.... down, five, six, seven, eight. Think of your body as a rubber band. Get nice and tall. Sky turn those toes out more. Again..."

"Ugggh! Ballet was rough today. Who can concentrate on *grand pliés* and ghost?" Sky asked, walking slowly into the foyer. Lola met her at the door, holding her little sister's hand as she waited for her mother to pick them up.

"Lola, are you staying for Modern

dance today?" asked Sky.

"No, my grandmother's coming to town and we have to get the house vacuumed and shiny. She does a white glove inspection for dust. It drives my mom crazy."

"Did you guys find anything?" Lola asked, chewing on her thumbnail.

"Nothing but an angry ghost. Lola, I think the house is actually haunted," Sky said. Lola's little sister, Zola, looked up at them with questions in her eyes.

"Mommy says there's no such thing as ghosts," Zola said softly. The kids looked at each other, silently agreeing not to scare the little girl.

"Well, we don't really know what we saw," said Nia. "We more heard things in the house. But it was pretty scary." Nia straightened the little girl's tutu and gave her a hug as their mother pulled up outside. Lola looked at all of them with concern.

"I know you guys are planning something. Be careful, ok?" Lola said as she left.

"Don't worry, Lola, we will be," Sky assured her. Zane met them in the mirrored room, his black tank partially hidden under a hoodie.

"What are we going to tell Ms. Kenya?" he asked.

"Nothing! She can't know we were there. She'll say it's dangerous, and maybe she'll start locking the door!" Sky hissed. Just as the kids had begun talking, Ms. Kenya came into the room. She stopped in front of the girls.

"Nia, what happened to your knee?" she asked, regarding the two flowered bandages that decorated the girl's injured knee.

Nia put her hands behind her back, unable to look her dance teacher

in the eye. "I, uh, I got hurt boarding, but I'm fine now," she said.

Ms. Kenya clucked her tongue and raised an eyebrow. "Nia, you know what I keep telling you about protecting your legs when you skateboard. Please wear a helmet, knee and elbow pads."

Nia nodded, and Ms. Kenya moved on to start the class. None of the kids could focus through the whole hour. As it ended, Ms. Kenya gave them more news.

"Everyone, I have a surprise!" she said. They all looked at her. She held up a pile of permission forms.

"I've arranged for us to have a sleepover party in the new place before we get going on the repairs! Don't worry; I've done a little dusting. This will help you guys get acquainted with the house. Won't that be fun?" she said.

Most of the others clapped with joy, but the girls exchanged a look of terror. They were going to spend a night in a haunted house?

Chapter Six

Kindness

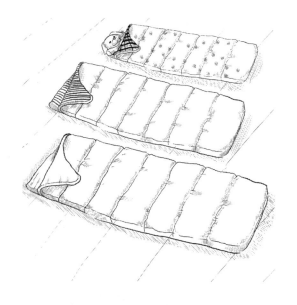

"This is going to be awful," Jada said, dragging her pink sleeping bag behind her into Mrs. Allen's old house.

"I don't think I'm going to sleep tonight. Especially not on this grimy floor." Nia said, checking the floor carefully for dirt before she laid out her own sleeping bag.

Sky laid hers out beside her. "No, you guys, this is perfect!" she said. Her friends eyed her like she had gone crazy. She rolled her eyes and opened her backpack, rummaging inside for something.

"I asked mom how to get rid of a pesky person. She said kindness could change most beings. People can be vile, mean and pesty because they need a friend. Ghosts used to be people so, it should work," Sky said.

"We are NOT trying that," Nia said immediately.

Sky yanked a flashlight out of her bag. "Why not? It won't hurt to be kind. Do you have a better idea?" she asked.

"No, but we don't want to get vanished," Jada said, hugging her stuffed bunny Flopsy to her chest.

"Who says we're going to get vanished? Maybe the ghost is afraid of us," Sky said.

Nia and Jada exchanged a look, and Nia reached out to feel Sky's forehead. "That's it. She's gone nuts."

Sky batted her hand away.

"So, what's the plan?" Zane asked as he laid out his camo sleeping bag.

Before Sky could explain her idea, Jada piped up. "Sky's going to try to make friends with the ghost," she said.

Zane looked at Sky with wide eyes. "Wow, you really are crazy to the tenth power," he said.

Sky glared at him. "Mom said it would work! And do you have a better idea?" she asked.

Zane smirked. "As a matter of fact,

I do." He opened his duffel bag and pulled something out of it.

Jada looked at it with caution. "A DirtBuster? Really, are we going to vacuum the ghost first and then ask it to leave?" she asked.

"Almost. You can suck ghosts up with these. I saw it in a movie," he said.

"You are such a nerd, Zane," Nia said, but she didn't object to this idea as much as she had to the first. A portable vacuum cleaner could come in handy.

"Mock me if you will, Nia, but this

stuff is very well documented," he said.

"Fine, whatever, bring your Dirt-Buster. We'll combine the plans. But we have to wait until everyone else goes to sleep," Sky said.

The friends settled in for a long night of waiting.

Chapter Seven

Brave

It was well past dark by the time the friends thought that everyone else was asleep. They stepped over the sleeping bodies of their friends and crept up the stairs for the third time that week. Instead of wandering around like before, they headed straight for the room at the end of the narrow hallway. Zane went first, his DirtBuster in front of him like a protective shield. They opened the door and found the room exactly as they had left it, minus the scratching noises and the terrifying moving sheet.

"What if it's not in here this time?" Zane whispered.

"Then we check all the rooms like we did last time," Sky whispered back.

"What if the ghost moves?" Jada asked. "There's no telling whether it would stay in one place. Do ghosts even sleep?"

Nia shrugged. "I don't know, but stop with all the questions. I'm trying to concentrate."

Just as they were about to check the other rooms, the scratching began again, along with a sound of thumping footsteps coming from the other side of the furniture.

"Shh! It's the ghost!" Sky hissed.

Zane pointed his DirtBuster towards the sound, but Sky made him lower it. "If we're going to make friends, we can't threaten it," she said.

Zane grumbled, but he kept the Dirt-Buster lowered. Sky climbed over a chair and stood on it.

"Sky, don't!" Jada said, but her friend was on a mission.

"Um, hello? Ghost? I, uh, was wondering if you wanted to, uh, talk?" she squeaked into the darkness.

The thumping got louder.

"Sky, let's go! I'm scared!" Nia said, grabbing Zane's arm. "Zane, do something!"

"Hello? Ghost?" Sky called again.

Zane came up beside the chair she

was standing on, the DirtBuster ready in his hand. "Sky, this was a really bad idea, let's just go."

As he tried to pull her off of the chair, Sky cupped her hands around her mouth and hissed, "GHOST! WE'RE NOT HERE TO HURT YOU! PLEASE COME OUT!"

Somewhere in the house a door closed and suddenly four ceiling tiles moved up and gently fell back into place. Everyone was frozen. How could ceiling move all by itself? The thumping got louder and louder, and suddenly, the far wall opened in a shower of plaster, dust and cobwebs. Jada and Nia screamed, and Zane yanked Sky back, brandishing his DirtBuster. A dark figure stood up, its tall wild hair almost brushing the top of the doorframe.

"What are you kids doing in here, yelling about ghosts?" A tall, lanky man with a full afro scrambled over the furniture and stood in front of them. The kids blinked up at him, shocked, as Ms. Kenya ran up the stairs, awakened by the screaming.

"Guys, what's going on up here?" she asked. She looked at the man. "Oh, Mr. Taylor. I thought you were here earlier," she said. The kids stared at their dance instructor.

"You know him?" Zane asked.

"Yes, this is Mr. Taylor. He's taken care of Mrs. Allen's property for over twenty years," Ms. Kenya said.

"So you know about the ghost? Can you help us make it move away?" Sky asked. The man looked down at her, his bushy mustache crinkling as he chuckled.

"Little lady, there's no ghost in this house," he said.

Jada tugged on his sleeve. "But Mr. Taylor, we all heard the scratching! And felt the whooshing! And we saw the sheets move! And just now the ceiling tiles moved like a giant was snoring and his breath sucked them up and then his *exhale* lowered them back into place," she said.

"My, my you guys have been on quite the adventure," said Ms. Kenya.

Mr. Taylor exchanged a look with Ms. Kenya. "I take it the little ones don't know about all of Mrs. Allen's wishes?" he said.

"I didn't think it was that important to tell them. I guess I should have thought about all of these wonderful imaginations," she said. The man walked over to the chair where they had seen the sheets move and pulled the cover off. A pair of sweet hedgehogs was curled in a hole in the upholstery, and three baby hedgehogs were nestled between them.

"Hedgehogs?" Zane asked, confused.

"Oh they're so cute. I want to hold them," Jada said.

"Yes, hedgehogs. I came back to feed them," Mr. Taylor said. "Just before she moved, Mrs. Allen said that no animals that I found in the house were to be killed, so I have to wait until

the babies are weaned and old enough before I can relocate them. The veterinarian comes by and checks on them."

"But what about the whooshing we felt earlier?" Sky asked.

"That old upstairs air conditioner has to be replaced. It either blows no air or big sudden puffs. Those puffs can knock a fellas hat off his head," Mr. Taylor replied.

"Well what about the moving ceiling tiles?" Nia asked.

"This house is big and drafty. Whenever the hallway door closes it creates an air pocket in the ceiling and sometimes the loose ceiling tiles move. It seems like I'd better glue them down tonight," laughed Mr. Taylor.

The kids turned to their dance instructor. "So there's no ghost? People won't be afraid to dance? We can move in here?" they asked.

"Of course we can. You all are so brave. You'll make great detectives," said Ms. Kenya, hugging them.

Story Bird Dance

Wordlist

Haunted Studio

Backdrops - A painted scenery hung at the back of a stage. The background of an event

Barre - The horizontal handrail placed at hip height. Dancers place their hands on for support during warm up and practice

Eerie -Uncanny. Strange and frightening

Exhale - Breathe out

First Position - A posture in which the feet are turned outward with the heels touching

Fortunate - Receiving good from uncertain or unexpected sources; lucky

Grand jete - A big jump in which a dancer leaps from one leg and lands on the other

Legacy - Transmitted by or received from the ancestors. Handed down from the past from a predecessor

Pirouette - Whirl or spin. A complete turn of the body on one foot

Pliés - Bending the knees and straightening them again, with the back straight. Often done with feet turned out. **Grand Pliés** - Bending of the knees until thighs are horizontal

Keep Reading

for a sneak peek at the next
Story Bird Dance adventure....

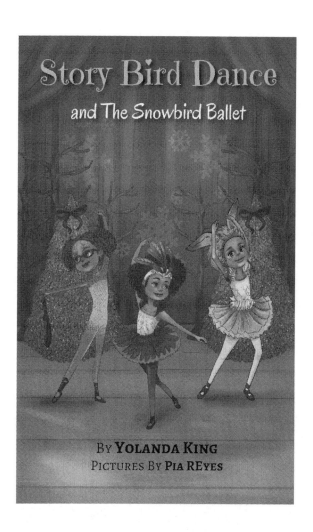

Chapter One
Letters

"I don't want to open it," Nia said,
sliding from the fluffy purple beanbag
onto the purple flower-shaped rug.
Her hands rested behind her touching
the wood floor. "What if I'm the Lizard

King? Open yours first," she said, nodding at Sky.

"Really Nia? You're going to let a little fear of reptiles keep you from dancing one of the best parts in the winter recital?" said Sky.

"Uh, yes," said Nia. "I like birds, rabbits, bears and dogs and cats and hamsters. I don't do scales."

Sky took a deep breath and shook her head. "Let's just wait for Jada and we'll open the letters together."

Ms. Kenya, the girls' dance teacher and owner of Story Bird Dance Academy, had mailed each student a letter announcing their parts in the winter recital. This was the school's first year performing during the winter. Ms. Kenya said she felt inspired by the coming cold days and decided to write and choreograph the modern ballet story The Snowbird for her students.

"Hey guys, so sorry I'm late," Jada said, rushing into the room. "My mom took forever finishing these two French braids. You'd think a psychologist would know better than trying to get the perfect center part." She dropped her coat onto the bed and pulled off

her hat. "What'd I miss?"

Nia patted a space next to her on the rug. She and Sky were sitting with their legs crossed. They both scooted to the edge of the rug and closer to the purple polka dot-covered bed.

"Well one, Nia is still afraid of crawly things with scales," said Sky. "Two, why are you wearing a wool hat when your mom just did your hair?"

"It's freezing outside and I don't want to catch a cold," said Jada. "I could miss school if I get sick. It's well documented that you have to protect your head and feet in the winter.

And Nia, I don't blame you. Sky, you remember those costume sketches Ms. Kenya showed us of the Lizard King costume? The glittery red, black and brown scales are lovely, but the crooked red hanging skin make me say ewww."

"That's what I was thinking, but I could totally rock the Snowbird, Arctic Hare or Polar Bear outfit. Feathers or fur look pretty good on me," said Nia. "But I think we can all cross out getting the Polar Bear parts. Zane or Ben will probably get them. Ms. Kenya has the bears lifting the hares during some of the leaps."

Sky sighed at both of her friends. "Ok ladies, let's get down to business. Jada did you bring your letter?"

"Sure did," said Jada waving her letter and sitting on the floor of Nia's room.

"Ok, on the count of three, everyone open your letter. One, two, three, open." The girls each broke the seal of their blue envelops and scanned the letters from Ms. Kenya.

Sky checked the faces of each of her closest friends, looking and hoping for the excitement she was feeling.

Ms. Kenya wrote several different characters into her ballet story. The Lizard King and Snowbird were the two leading *antagonist* and *protagonist* characters. The Polar Bears and Arctic Hares had a major dance battle scene with the Lizard King and his minions, the Leaf Lizards.

She was just about to ask her friends what their parts were when Nia's mom poked her head in the door and asked, "Anyone want to try some hot chai tea and ginger peppermint cookies? I know today is a big day." The girls loved going to Nia's house. Her mom had a pastry *catering* business and was constantly experimenting with different cookie recipes. This winter she was adding teas to her business.

"Thank you, Mrs. Starr," the girls called out in unison. Mrs. Starr set a tray in front of the girls and kissed the top of Nia's head and gave the other girls a quick head massage. "I wasn't always a mom and cookie expert. My college dance professor always reminded us that the most important thing is that you get better each time you practice."

"Yes ma'am," the girls said, as Nia's mom left the purple bedroom.

"Ok guys, who wants to go first?" said Sky.

30158534R00048

Made in the USA
Columbia, SC
26 October 2018